THE AMAZING ADVENTURES OF THE DC SUPER-PETS!

Cave of Kryptonite!

by **Steve Korté**

illustrated by **Art Baltazar**

Superman created by Jerry Siegel
and Joe Shuster
by special arrangement with
the Jerry Siegel Family

PICTURE WINDOW BOOKS
a capstone imprint

Published by Picture Window Books, an imprint of Capstone.
1710 Roe Crest Drive
North Mankato, Minnesota 56003
www.capstonepub.com

Cataloging-in-Publication Data is available at the Library of Congress website.
ISBN: 978-1-5158-7176-7 (library binding)
ISBN: 978-1-5158-7321-1 (paperback)
ISBN: 978-1-5158-7184-2 (eBook PDF)

Summary: A game of hide-and-seek turns deadly as Superman and his
Kryptonian canine, Krypto, are faced with rescues that challenge even the
mightiest of heroes. Will the Man of Steel and his Super-dog save the day?

Designed by Ted Williams
Design Elements by Shutterstock/SilverCircle

Printed in the United States   3881

TABLE OF CONTENTS

He is Superman's
loyal friend.
He came from the
planet Krypton.
He and the Man of Steel share
many of the same superpowers.
These are . . .

THE AMAZING
ADVENTURES OF

Krypto the
Super-Dog!

CHAPTER 1

Hide-and-Seek

Superman and Krypto are playing a game of hide-and-seek. They are high above the city of Metropolis.

The Man of Steel is holding Krypto's favorite chew toy. It's a large lead pipe. Krypto's jaws are so strong that he destroys ordinary dog toys.

"Close your eyes and count to 20!" Superman says to the happy Super-Dog.

Superman flies through the air to a cave inside a mountain.

"Krypto will have to use his X-ray vision to find the pipe inside this cave," says Superman.

Suddenly, Superman feels weak. He sees a small, glowing green rock. It is stuck in the wall of the cave. The green rock is Kryptonite! It's the one thing that can harm Superman.

The Man of Steel falls to the ground.

He can't move.

Krypto dashes to the front of the cave.

"Woof!" he says. He is eager to find

his toy.

"Krypto, don't get too close," warns
Superman. "The Kryptonite will harm
you too!"

What made that noise?

Superman uses his X-ray vision to
look through the top of the cave.

He sees a rocket flying high above the mountain. The rocket is covered in bright red flames. It is falling toward the ground.

"Krypto, stop the rocket!" says Superman.

WHOOSH!

The Super-Dog soars through the air. He grabs one wing of the rocket in his powerful jaws.

Krypto slows the falling rocket and brings it safely down.

Superman is still trapped. Krypto stands outside the cave. The Super-Dog looks worried.

CHAPTER 2

Free Fall!

From far away, someone is yelling for help. Superman uses his super-hearing. The voice is coming from high up on the mountain.

"Krypto, I need you to investigate," says the Man of Steel.

The Super-Dog flies high in the air. He sees a man who has stumbled and fallen off the hiking path. The man is hanging onto the edge of a cliff.

"Help!" yells the man.

Just then, the man loses his grip and starts to fall.

The Super-Dog zooms into action. He
flies in circles around the man, soaring
faster and faster.

Krypto creates a pocket of air around the man. Thanks to Krypto's fast thinking, the man floats safely to the ground.

Now it's time to rescue Superman!

CHAPTER 3

Superpowered Pup

BLAM!

Krypto crashes into the cave's roof.

He has to destroy the Kryptonite to save

Superman! The cave shakes on impact.

The chunk of Kryptonite breaks into tiny bits of green powder.

Krypto wags his tail super-fast. The motion of his tail creates a windstorm. It blows the dangerous green powder far away from Superman.

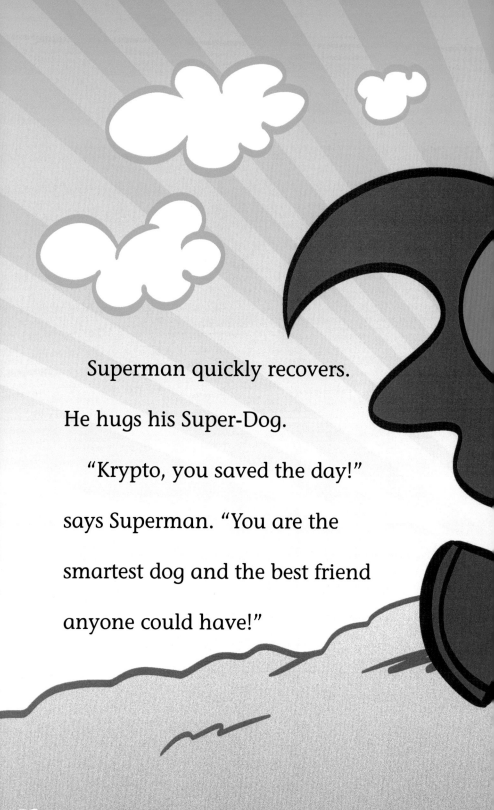

Superman quickly recovers.

He hugs his Super-Dog.

"Krypto, you saved the day!"

says Superman. "You are the

smartest dog and the best friend

anyone could have!"

AUTHOR!

Steve Korté is the author of many books for children and young adults. He worked at DC Comics for many years, editing more than 600 books about Superman, Batman, Wonder Woman, and the other heroes and villains in the DC Universe. He lives in New York City with his husband, Bill, and their super-cat, Duke.

ILLUSTRATOR!

Famous cartoonist Art Baltazar is the creative force behind *The New York Times* bestselling, Eisner Award-winning DC Comics' Tiny Titans; co-writer for Billy Batson and the Magic of Shazam, Young Justice, Green Lantern Animated (Comic); and artist/co-writer for the awesome Tiny Titans/Little Archie crossover, Superman Family Adventures, Super Powers, and Itty Bitty Hellboy! Art is one of the founders of Aw Yeah Comics comic shop and the ongoing comic series! Aw yeah, living the dream! He stays home and draws comics and never has to leave the house! He lives with his lovely wife, Rose, sons Sonny and Gordon, and daughter Audrey! AW YEAH MAN! Visit him at www.artbaltazar.com

"Word Power"

chunk (CHUHNK)—a solid piece of something

cliff (KLIF)—a high, steep rock face

eager (EE-guhr)—very excited and interested

impact (IM-pakt)—two objects coming together with great force

investigate (in-VESS-tuh-gate)—to find out as much as possible about an event or a person

recover (ree-KUH-vuhr)—to return to a normal state of health, mind, or strength

stumble (STUHM-buhl)—to trip or fall

X-ray vision (EKS-ray VIZH-uhn)—the ability to see inside a person or through objects

WRITING PROMPTS

1. Superman is helpless because of Kryptonite. Write your own story about how the Kryptonite ended up in the cave.

2. Do you have a pet? What if it had superpowers? Write a story with you as the hero and your pet as a sidekick!

3. Pretend you are the hiker Krypto rescued. How would you retell the story to your friends?

DISCUSSION QUESTIONS

1. Krypto and Superman share many of the same powers. Which power—or powers—would you like to have? How would you use them for good?

2. Why is Krypto's toy a lead pipe? What do you think would happen if Superman gave Krypto a regular dog toy?

3. Where did the rocket come from? What was it doing before it crashed? Come up with several different ideas. Then compare them with a friend.

THE AMAZING ADVENTURES OF THE DC SUPER-PETS!

Collect them all!